Jack *the* runaway terrier

By Gill Mclean

Down in the valley, between farm and stream,
Stands a little stone cottage
with low hanging beams,

Where a small dog lies dreaming of rabbits and trees,
Whilst another is sniffing the scent on the breeze.

No, Jack is not sleeping, his eye on the door,
For Jack loves to wander,
He loves to explore.

So out in all weathers his owner must go,
To search for that dog in the wind, rain and snow.

Jack loves to chase pheasants
and rabbits and foxes.
He loves to scare chickens
upon their nest boxes.

The farmer could rant
and the game keeper roar.
Jack's owner would scold him
and send him indoors.

But given a chance he'll be out on the run,
Because Jack loves adventure - for him it is fun.
So when the wind blows and the door opens wide,
He seizes the moment and scampers outside.

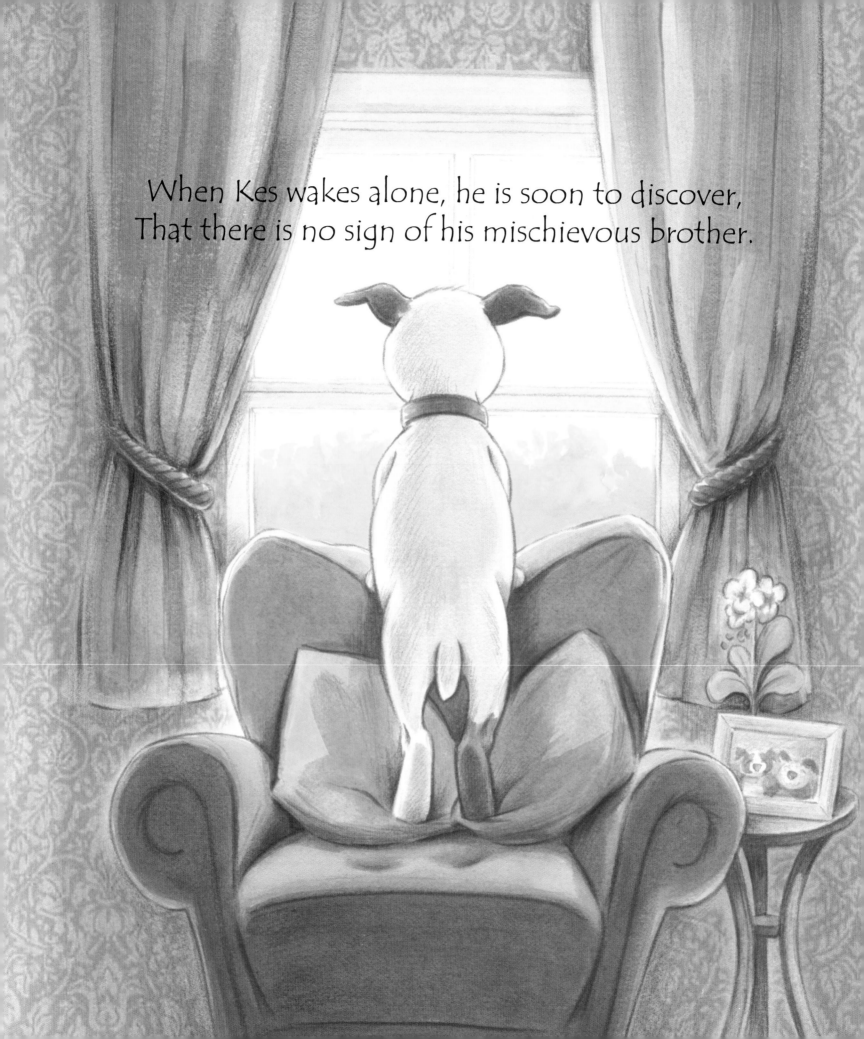

When Kes wakes alone, he is soon to discover,
That there is no sign of his mischievous brother.

His owner could call and his owner could plead,
But there is no answer, for Jack will not heed.

For what could be better
than sniffing the air?

His owner is begging, but what could he care?

Down past the cowsheds,
along the stone wall,

Out through the meadow, away from her call.

Into the woods and over the road,
Young Jack simply follows his terrier nose.

Then over a hill top he sees with delight,
A huddle of roof tops, a sea sparkling bright.
A broad open ocean, "Ah, freedom!" He cries,
But an ocean is deep, and an ocean is wide.

And though the sea glitters and beckons him near,
Away from the shoreline a small cloud appears.

The harbour is busy, the town is so loud,
A small dog is very soon lost in the crowd.

Down at the jetty are boats of all sizes,
Such colours and smells and endless surprises.

Jack watches the fishermen ready the boat,
Busy with lobster pots, fishing nets, ropes.

By the time they have noticed the dog on the deck,
The harbour and town is a vanishing speck.

So the crew let him stay
and they pat his small back,
And they laugh when he barks
at the gulls and the crabs.

But the clouds, they have gathered
and brew high above,
And the winds chase the storm
to the boat soon enough.

The sparkly sea has turned solemn grey.
The wind licks the churning waves, whipping up spray.
The sea heaves the boat and the waves splash the deck.
The rain beats down hard
on Jack's back and his neck.

And Jack whispers quietly under his breath, "I wish I was at home with my brother, Kes."

Back at the cottage the curtains are drawn,
The fire is blazing, the sitting room warm,
And Kes snuggles up with his owner and sighs.
Is Jack cold and hungry, beneath open skies?

For three days and nights
Jack longs for dry land,
When finally reaching it,
he barely can stand.

His coat is all matted,
his ribs showing through.
His rascally spirit is sorely subdued.

So turning his back on the harbour and town,
Over the hilltop; take the road down.

Back through the meadow, along the stone wall.
At last to the cow sheds and finally home.

Alone on the doorstep he fears the worst.
Am I forgotten, and given up for lost?

But Kes hears Jack's voice and he barks his reply,

"The ocean is deep and the ocean is wide."

Though Jack loves to wander and Jack loves to roam,
He never does venture too far from his home.

His brother is with him wherever they go,
And always, but always,
their owner in tow.

Jack the Runaway Terrier

First published in 2019 in Great Britain by
Banana Boat Books

the picture books imprint of

Monkey Island Publishing
Dairy Cottage
Hurgill Road
Richmond
North Yorkshire
DL10 4SZ

ISBN 978 0 9933079 1 1

A CIP catalogue record of this book is available from the British library

Printed in Malta

MONKEY*ISLAND
PUBLISHING